Wow! CREATION

**For Luca and Phoebe:
Imagination opens up a whole new world.
Never stop exploring and creating.
You don't know what you'll discover next.**

Published by
Candle Books
www.spckpublishing.co.uk
Part of the SPCK Group
Society for Promoting Christian Knowledge, Studio 101, The Record Hall,
16–16A Baldwin's Gardens, London EC1N 7RJ, UK

ISBN 978 1 78128 466 7

First edition 2025

Acknowledgments
Scripture quotations are taken from the Holy Bible, New Living Translation, copyright © 1996. Used by permission of Tyndale House Publishers, Inc., Carol Stream, Illinois 60189, USA. All rights reserved.

A catalogue record for this book is available from the British Library
Printed and bound in China by Dream Colour (Hong Kong) Printing Ltd

Produced on paper from sustainable sources

Wow! CREATION

Creatively explore being green for God's creation

MARTHA SHRIMPTON

ILLUSTRATED BY SARAH NOLLOTH

The Wow! Series

Connect creatively with your maker, your family, and your community with this series of books exploring stories and themes found in the Bible.

Wow! Hello, Creative Explorer! I am so glad that you have joined me on this mission to unpack God's awesome creation! What an exciting journey there is ahead! So, grab the rest of your creative team (friends and family) because we are about to dive into this story by playing, celebrating, and creating! Let's go!

Pray || Pause || Play || Create || Celebrate || Communicate

PRAY

Wow! Hello God . . . Opportunities to pray in a creative way, by yourself or with others.

PAUSE

Wow! Time to pause . . . Take some time out to reflect on an element of creation, and how it fits with your life now.

PLAY

Wow! What a show . . . Ideas to get you on your feet and having a bit of fun around the theme.

CREATE

Wow! Let's create! Fun crafts and creations that help you to explore some of the story's themes.

CELEBRATE

Wow! That's cool! Celebrate God's creation and find ways to praise him for his gift to us.

COMMUNICATE

Wow! Can we chat? A chance to chat and connect with each other, using parts of the theme as conversation starters.

TOP TIP!

At the start of each chapter, you will spot a passage reference to find in your Bible. This will lead you to the story we will be exploring together! So, why not read the story in your Bible before you start your creative journey?

For more creative resources, visit the Nimbus Collective website at www.nimbuscollective.org

Nimbus Collective is an organization founded by Martha Shrimpton. It is aimed at helping you to connect in a creative way with yourself and God.

Contents

The Creator's Creation!

God owns and made everything in the world

PSALM 24

THE EARTH AND EVERYTHING IN IT . . .
The WHOLE world, the sea, and the skies . . .
the trees, the grass, the flowers . . .
The seasons, the weather . . .
The tops of the mountains and the very bottom of the ocean . . .
The ground for the plants' roots and the clouds that hold the rain . . .
The people, the animals, and EVERY living thing . . .

IT ALL BELONGS TO GOD!
Lift up your eyes and look at THE CREATOR OF EVERYTHING!

Wow! God made the earth and everything in it!

Want to read more of David's psalm of praise?
Why not dive into your Bible and read **PSALM 24?**

Or . . . you could start your creative adventure right away!

SHAKE IT UP!

Wow! God created the world and EVERYTHING in it!

He also made sure that all the basic stuff was ready before even starting on the rest of his creation! Just so that everything would be perfect.

DID YOU KNOW?

The surface of the earth is 71% water and only 29% land!

The ocean bed needed to be made really secure to hold all that water!

Let's get creative!

Create a "Globe Prayer Globe" to remind you of God's awesome creation of the world and the universe.

YOU WILL NEED:

a jam jar
a ping-pong ball
green and blue paint or pens
sequins or glitter
water

STEP 1 Decorate the ping-pong ball with green and blue paint to make it look like the earth.

STEP 2 Place the painted ball in the jam jar. Also put in the sequins and glitter (these will be all the stars in the universe).

STEP 3 Fill the jar with water and put the lid on tightly.

STEP 4 Shake the globe and look at the stars whizzing around the earth. Say a prayer to thank God for his creation as you watch it spin.

Wow! Time to pause . . .

HEAD TOWARD **THE SON**

A sunflower's head faces toward the rising sun in the morning and follows the sun as it moves throughout the day!

God created the sun, the largest light in the sky. God also sent Jesus to earth to be "the light of the world". Jesus brightens up our lives by giving us the gift of being friends with God! He shows us who God is!

Let's get creative!

YOU WILL NEED:

a sunflower seed
soil
a plant pot
water (to water your plant!)

Plant a sunflower seed in some new soil.

As it slowly grows, ask God to help you to keep your eyes on him. Ask him to remind you that Jesus is the light of the world, and that he gives everyone joy and hope in their lives.

NOT WEEDS . . . WILD FLOWERS!

So many people think that weeds are a pest in the garden! However, many weeds are actually beautiful wild flowers! They are bright with varied shapes and are stunning to look at throughout the whole year.

Pretend that you are a presenter on a gardening show on TV.

Create an episode where you tell the audience that weeds are not a bad thing. They are beautiful and bright and attract so many different animals and pollinators.

Explain that they were designed and created by God. You could even add a part where you show people different wild flowers that you have found yourself.

When you have created your episode, why not perform your show to someone?

DID YOU KNOW?

The daisy is one of the most common wild flowers and has been around since at least 2200 BC, when the Egyptians were known to grow them as medicine!

A LEAF WREATH!

God designed so many different light and dark shades in creation to show us his creativity! There's golden orange, deep red, forest green, and even rich purple too. Go and step outside. How many different shades can you see in nature? It's time to celebrate God's creativity!

Let's get creative!

Let's create a beautiful leaf wreath!

YOU WILL NEED:

wire
an outdoor space to forage

STEP 1

Collect lots of different leaves and petals. Find them on the ground or on wild trees. Make sure you only gather from places where you have permission to do so.

STEP 2

Ask an adult to bend your wire into a circle, leaving a good amount for the hook at the top.

STEP 3

Thread your foraged leaves and petals onto the wire until it is full!

STEP 4

Twist the top to secure it and make a loop to hang the wreath up!

STEP 5

Hang it on your door to celebrate the beauty God gives us in nature!

MAKE A JOYFUL NOISE!

WOW! God really made EVERYTHING in this world! What an awesome God!

Psalm 24 was written by David as a song to be sung to praise God. Why not praise God for his creation with your own music?

Let's get creative!

Let's use some of God's creation to create musical instruments and make joyful sounds of praise to him.

STEP 1 Collect lots of different objects from outside: sticks, logs, leaves, rocks, and anything else you can find.

STEP 2 Try scraping, bashing, tapping, and scrunching the objects to make sounds and rhythms.

STEP 3 While you joyfully play your nature instruments, thank God for how amazing he is and for the gift of nature he has given us!

MUSIC TO GOD'S EARS

Creation is one of the best gifts God has given us! Incredible tall trees! Calming gentle waterfalls! Golden yellow sunrises! Friends who make us laugh from our bellies!

What other beautiful things in creation can you think of?

Let's get creative!

Why not write your own song of praise just like David did in Psalm 24?

Write or draw a picture of the parts of creation and nature that you want to thank God for.

When you have thought of your ideas, sing each line to a tune you know. If you're feeling really creative, you could make up a melody of your own.

Thank you, God, for . . .

The Ultimate Gift!

God asks us to take care of his creation

GENESIS 1 – 2

At first, there was nothing: no light, no sound.
Only God could be found.
On Day 1, he spoke out loudly. LET THERE BE LIGHT!
And there was day and night.
AND IT WAS GOOD!
On Day 2, he separated the sea and sky.
The sparkling waves crashed nearby.
AND IT WAS GOOD!
On Day 3, he separated the land from the sea.
He filled the ground with luscious greenery.
AND IT WAS GOOD!
On Day 4, he made the moon and sun
and twinkling stars. God was having fun!
AND IT WAS GOOD!
On Day 5, he filled the ocean with many sea creatures,
and birds flew in the sky with all kinds of features!
AND IT WAS GOOD!
On Day 6, he moulded wildlife and anything that crawls.
The earth was filled with plenty of humans and animals!
AND IT WAS **VERY** GOOD!

Wow! God really is the **ULTIMATE** creator!

Want to read more about what happened when God created the earth?
Why not dive into your Bible and read **GENESIS 1 AND 2?**

Or . . . you could start your creative adventure right away!

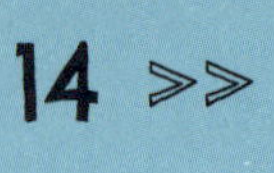

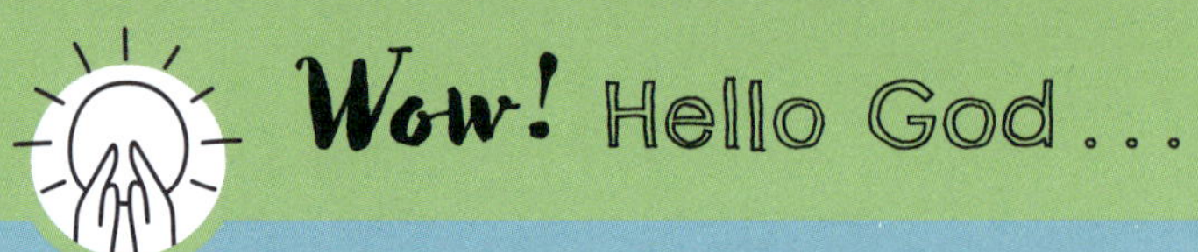

PLANT A PRAYER

Isn't it cool that God put humans in charge of looking after the land? That means that even *now* he has put *us* in charge of the whole earth. That includes taking care of all the trees, plants, animals, and everything that grows!

Let's get creative!

Why not make some "Wood Stick Prayers" and plant them outside?

Write a simple prayer about the needs of the plants, animals, and natural habitats (places) on a wooden stick. This could be a one-word prayer such as "Protect" or "Nourish", or a longer prayer, asking him to help us to be wise with how we look after the land, animals, and plants.

GROWTH

SHELTER

NOURISH

I'LL GET YOU A DRINK

Why not create a rain jar to collect rainwater so you can give the plants that God made the most nourishing water possible? You can then water them with the rainwater collected on a day when it has not rained!

DID YOU KNOW?

Plants prefer rainwater to water from the tap because it has more of the nutrients (goodness) they need to help them to grow!

Let's get creative!

YOU WILL NEED:

a large plastic bottle
scissors
tape

TOP TIP: You may need to ask an adult to help you to cut the top of the bottle off.

STEP 1 Draw a line around the top of the widest part of the bottle. Cut around the whole of this line.

STEP 2 Turn the neck of the bottle upside down to sit inside the bottle as a funnel. Tape the two sections of the bottle together.

STEP 3 You could decorate the outside of the bottle with stickers or pens to make it bright and striking!

STEP 4 Dig a small dip in the ground to secure your bottle outside or wedge it in between two rocks so it won't fall over.

STEP 5 Wait for the rain to come and collect in your bottle!

Rain collecting is a slow process and it forces you to take your time. However, the nutrients in rainwater are hugely valuable to our plants, so it is definitely worth the wait!

I NAME YOU . . .

In Genesis 2, God put Adam in charge of naming the animals on the earth. Some types of animal have very funny names, like the "sparklemuffin", the "blue-footed booby", and the "star-nosed mole"! They all really exist!

What names would you give to animals if you were Adam? Would it be something totally ridiculous just to make everyone laugh?

Let's act!

Create a scene where you play the part of Adam.

In the scene, you are given animals to name that are very strange-looking! They have the most outrageous noses and an unbelievable amount of legs, and make the most bizarre noises you have ever heard!

Once you have created your scene, why not show it to friends and family to make them laugh too!

TOP TIP: Draw your strange animal in the space below to inspire your scene!

A MINI HAVEN

When God created the garden of Eden in Genesis 2, it was the most beautiful, exotic garden ever seen. It was full of bright flowers, flourishing trees and bushes, and all kinds of animals!

Have a go at creating your own beautiful mini garden for all different insects to enjoy!

Let's get creative!

YOU WILL NEED:

a small bowl or plant pot that is not used any more

STEP 1 Fill the bottom of the bowl with stones and soil.

STEP 2 Collect small plant shoots, moss, leaves, and any other interesting natural objects you can find in the garden, such as acorns or bark.

STEP 3 Arrange these objects in your bowl to create a mini garden.

STEP 4 Leave it outside as a haven for insects to explore and enjoy!

LONG BEAK, LOOKING CHIC

Aren't the different shapes, sizes, and patterns of animals incredible?! God obviously had A LOT of fun creating all the different types of animals! They're not just made to look funny for no reason, though: God designed them that way for a purpose!

Some animals have very long bills, such as the platypus! This is to help them find delicious food in deep mud. Some have very large eyes, such as tarsiers, to give them superpowered nighttime vision!

Let's get creative!

In the space below, design a funny-looking animal of your own! You could take inspiration from some of God's unique-looking creatures!

TOP TIP: **Use these questions to help inspire your creation.**

Where does the animal live? Maybe it needs fur, scales, or something else.

What does the animal eat? Maybe it needs a special body part to find food.

What does it do in the day? Maybe it needs something to help it swim or see in the dark too!

Give thanks to God and celebrate the amazing features each one of his animals has! Ask God to help us to know how to look after these animals, as well as the places where they live.

STOP AND SMELL THE HERBS

God not only created beautiful-looking plants, he also made sure they had a distinct smell and taste! Humans love to enjoy them.

However, it's not only humans that love these plants. Bees and other insects do, too! These plants provide food and pollen for things that crawl, scurry, wriggle, and fly! These creatures then help to keep our soil healthy, pollinate crops, and so much more!

Let's get creative!

Choose a few different herbs that you like and plant them into a pot to keep on your windowsill.

As the plant flourishes and grows, rub and smell the leaves. Breathe in deeply and enjoy the smell. Keep an eye out for any insects you can see on the plants. What do they look like? Do they move fast or slowly?

In the spaces below, draw or write an answer to each statement.

The smell of this plant makes me feel . . .

The texture of this plant reminds me of . . .

The shape of this plant makes me think . . .

The taste of this plant is . . .

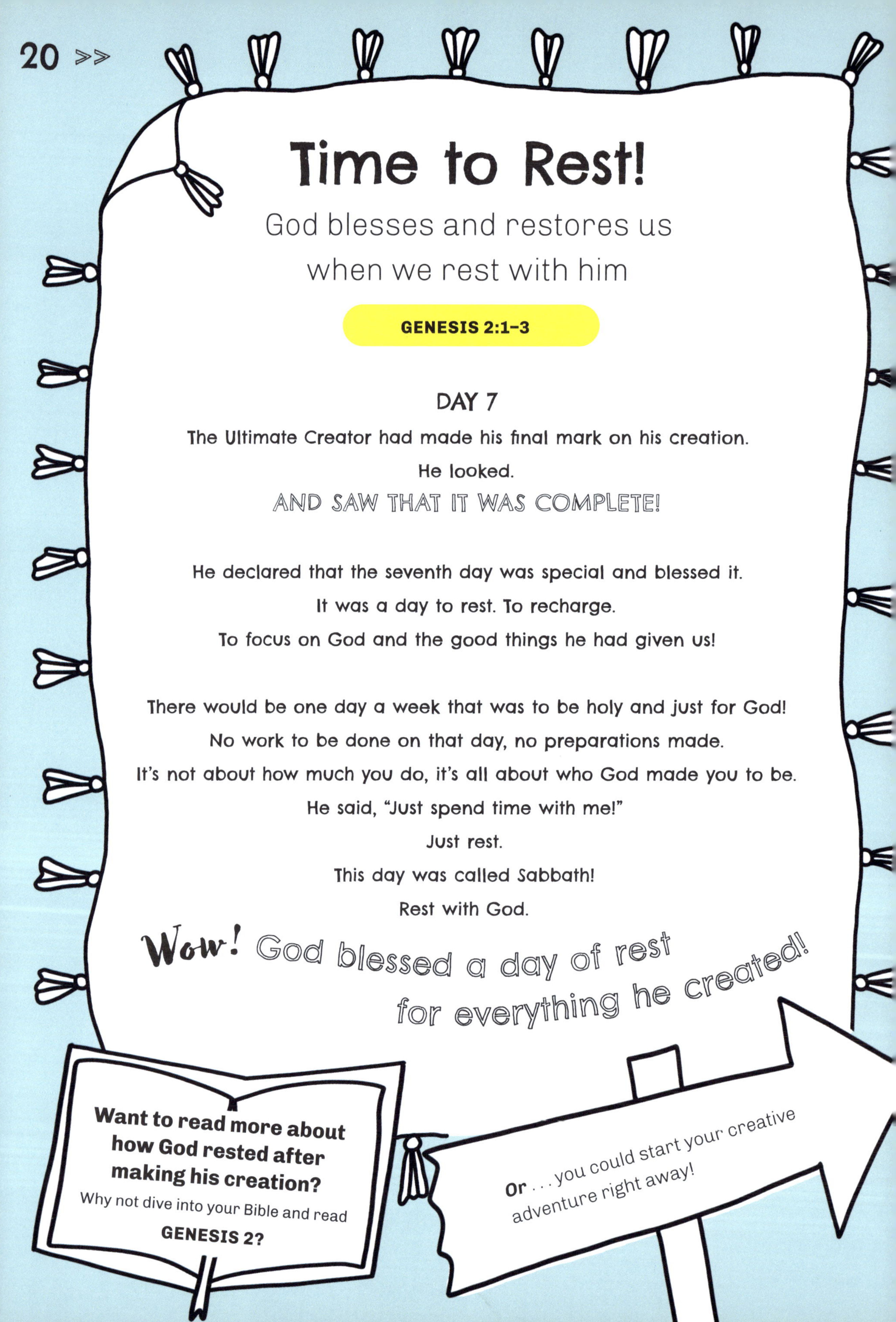

Time to Rest!

God blesses and restores us when we rest with him

GENESIS 2:1–3

DAY 7

The Ultimate Creator had made his final mark on his creation.

He looked.

AND SAW THAT IT WAS COMPLETE!

He declared that the seventh day was special and blessed it.

It was a day to rest. To recharge.

To focus on God and the good things he had given us!

There would be one day a week that was to be holy and just for God!

No work to be done on that day, no preparations made.

It's not about how much you do, it's all about who God made you to be.

He said, "Just spend time with me!"

Just rest.

This day was called Sabbath!

Rest with God.

Wow! God blessed a day of rest for everything he created!

Want to read more about how God rested after making his creation?

Why not dive into your Bible and read **GENESIS 2?**

Or . . . you could start your creative adventure right away!

IRIDESCENT SIGHT

God breathes life into us and blesses us with a massive variety of flowers and animals! The land looks really bright!

Bubble prayers can really help to remind us of this blessing!

DID YOU KNOW?

Bubbles change their look depending on how thick the water is on the bubble walls, and light hitting the bubbles gives them an iridescent glow. Iridescent means that the bubble seems to change depending on the angle you look at it from!

YOU WILL NEED:

tub of bubble liquid with wand

STEP 1 As you gently blow air into a bubble, think of God giving us our first breath.

STEP 2 Trace the path of the bubble with your finger.

STEP 3 Look at its changing, glowing surface as it gracefully falls.

STEP 4 As you watch the bubble, say this prayer:

Thank you, God, for the breath you give me and how boldly you formed the earth!

Help me to slow down, like this bubble, and notice all the blessings you have given me.

Amen.

BREATHE IN, BREATHE OUT

We can realize just how amazing God's work is simply by looking at the incredible things God designed in our body and how it all works together.

He wants us to take time to pause and rest, just like he did! He blessed the day of rest and made it holy: the day was called Sabbath.

DID YOU KNOW?

Your heart beats around 100,000 times a day, and you breathe in and out around 22,000 times a day!

Let's pause!

Hold your hand in front of your body and spread your fingers out wide.

Use your index finger on one hand to trace your fingers on the other hand.

As you trace up, breathe in, and as you trace down, breathe out.

As you breathe in, in your head ask God to be with you.

As you breathe out, in your head ask God to restore you and give you peace.

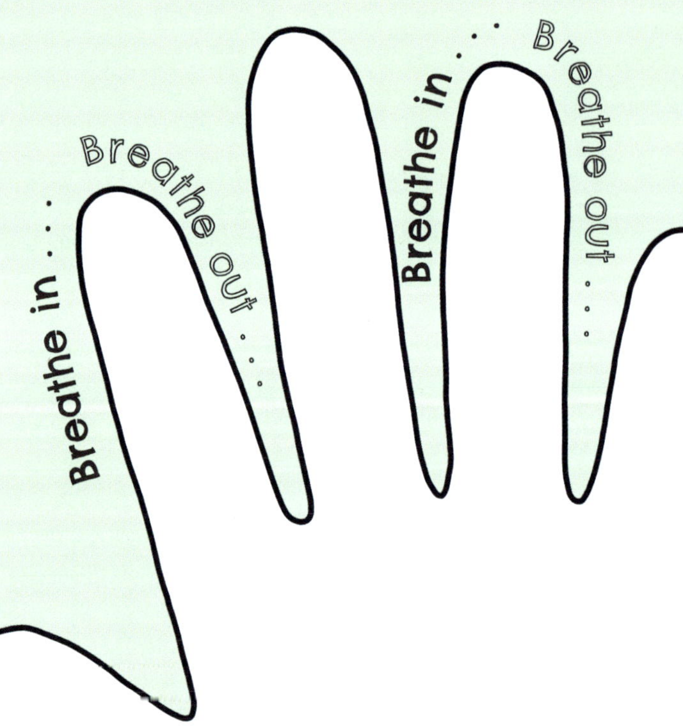

WHAT! NO CROP!?

As humans, we can often want to overuse the land God gives us. We want to build more houses, and produce more food and crops, than the land can handle!

In the story in Genesis, God takes a day just to rest! However, God knew that the land needed to rest too, and to revive! Once rested, the land often produces more and better crops!

DID YOU KNOW?

Farmers use a technique called "fallow land" when farming.

This is when a part of land that is usually used for farming has no crops planted in it for one whole season. This helps the soil to recover and develop all the nutrients (goodness) it needs for the next crop!

Let's act!

Ask a friend to help you to create a scene between two farmers.

In the scene, improvise a conversation between the two characters about leaving the land to rest as fallow land.

One person plays the role of a shocked farmer, who is outraged that there is no crop to be planted.

The other farmer must convince him or her that, by leaving the land fallow, more crops will be produced next season.

TOP TIP

Once you have finished creating your scene, why not find someone to perform to!

FLOWER FOOD

God wants good things for us and for his creation! He helps us to take care of the plants and to make sure they have all the nutrients they need to flourish, simply by giving us ways to make the soil really good for them!

Let's get creative!

You can make the soil in your garden or plant pots really healthy by giving the ground a little bit of help. All you need is some natural compost to restore goodness in the soil!

It takes time to make compost and you need to be willing to wait patiently, but it holds so many good nutrients that are good for the plants!

Wear gardening gloves

YOU WILL NEED:

a large bucket

STEP 1 Gather fallen leaves and grass cuttings from the ground.

STEP 2 Break up all the leaves into small pieces and place all that you've gathered into the bucket.

STEP 3 Cover the bucket, leave it at the bottom of the garden, and wait for the pieces to break down into compost.

STEP 4 When it is damp and sludge-like, mix the compost with soil to make a new mixture.

STEP 5 Use this to plant new flowers in pots or top up the soil in existing beds in your garden.

IT TAKES ITS TIME!

The awesome thing about nature is that it doesn't rush things! The golden sun rises slowly and makes its way gently around the globe as the glistening moon leisurely shows its face. A flower gradually unfolds its petals, one by one.

Nature takes its time but always gives us more than we could imagine when it arrives!

Let's get creative!

Create your own time-lapse flick-book showing the sun rising!

YOU WILL NEED:

multiple small pieces of paper of the same size
a stapler
pens and pencil crayons

STEP 1 Pile all your small pieces of paper on top of one another and staple one side so they don't move.

STEP 2 On the first page, draw a horizon without the sun.

STEP 3 On the next page, draw the exact same line for your horizon and add a small arch showing the sun beginning to rise over the land.

STEP 4 Repeat this on each page, each time drawing a little more of the sun showing over the skyline. Continue until the whole sun is above the land.

STEP 5 Flick the book from front to back. You should be able to see your sun rise from picture to picture!

TOP TIP
Complete each picture by showing how the light changes as the sun rises. You could look at pictures of sunrises to inspire you.

FAR AND NEAR, WHAT CAN YOU HEAR?

It isn't just our eyes that can appreciate the wonders of nature! There are also so many different sounds, from twittering birds to whipping wind, from the crunch of leaves underfoot to the pitter-patter of rain in the distance.

Let's pause!

With an adult, go for a walk in nature away from busy roads or places full of people. This could be in the woods or fields or even by a river.

Stand with your eyes closed and begin to listen to the noises around you.

What is the furthest noise you can hear?

As you listen, notice the noise you can hear closest to you and share this with your friend.

Together, name and count all the different noises you can hear in nature. Don't rush, take your time to listen.

Thank God for the gift of different senses, helping you to appreciate nature.

A Big Promise!

God promises he will care for and love his creation

GENESIS 6 – 9

God wasn't so happy with the people on earth.
They were not looking after the land, or the creatures, or even one another!
He decided that he wanted to start again, and chose
one man and his family to help him out.

Noah.
"Go and build a giant boat! An ark!" cried God to Noah.
"Make it big enough to carry all your family and two of every animal!"

So Noah set to work! He sawed and hammered, nailed
and sanded, until the giant boat was built!

Noah gathered his family and the animals and
guided them onto his floating masterpiece!

God shut the door and they heard a noise on the roof.

Drip. Drop. Splash. Splosh.

God sent the rain! It rained and poured and the land flooded!

The rain fell for 40 days. Until God said, "ENOUGH!" He stopped the rain and,
once the land had dried up, invited Noah and his family safely out of the ark.

As Noah looked out onto the empty land, he noticed
a bright, bold rainbow form in the sky.

"I PROMISE . . ." God spoke, ". . . that I will NEVER do this again! I
will look after you! I will care for you and for all your children.
Go and enjoy the land! Take care of it! Multiply and fill it!"

Wow! What an amazing promise God made!

Want to read more about this story of Noah and God?
Why not dive into your Bible and read **GENESIS 6 – 9?**

Or . . . you could start your creative adventure right away!

HIDDEN BLESSINGS

God sent a rainbow to remind people that he promised to take care of all the earth and everything in it. He even blessed Noah and his sons, saying they would have more blessings to come! These blessings are for you too!

In the same way that God sent a reminder of his blessings in the sign of a rainbow, why not create your own hidden sign for people to be reminded of God's love?

Let's get creative!

With an adult, walk around the area where you live and take a piece of chalk with you.

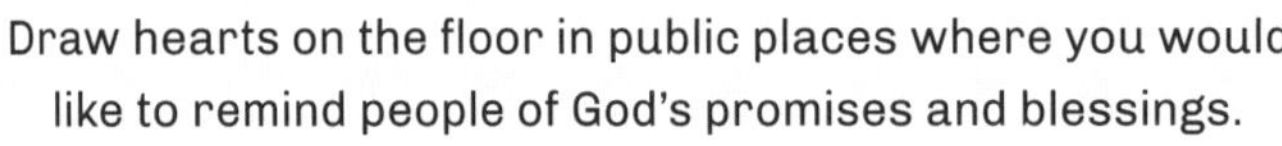
Draw hearts on the floor in public places where you would like to remind people of God's promises and blessings.

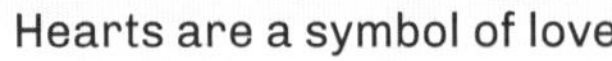
Hearts are a symbol of love.

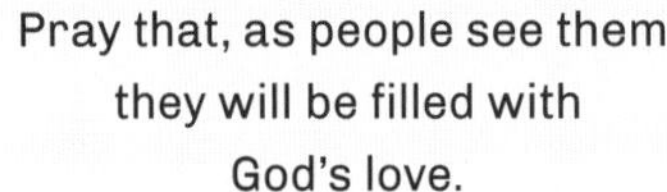

Pray that, as people see them, they will be filled with God's love.

A CLOUD WITH SILVER LINING

The great Flood seemed like quite a bad situation for Noah and his family. They were stuck in the ark for a very long time, even after it kept raining for a full 40 days! Until, one day, Noah's dove flew back to the ark carrying a leaf. The water that had flooded the earth was gone. It was exactly the "silver lining" they needed!

DID YOU KNOW?

The phrase, "Every cloud has a silver lining," means, "No matter how bad a situation is, there is always good to be found."

Let's pause!

Take some time to do a little cloud-gazing.

STEP 1 Lie on the ground outside or on the floor near a window and breathe in deeply. As you lie still, watch the clouds go by slowly.

STEP 2 What shapes can you see? How many shades are there?

STEP 3 How many of them have a dark silver line on the bottom?

When you spot a cloud with a silver lining, why not thank God that he always gives us good things to find in every situation?

HAVE YOU HEARD THE NEWS?

It would have been so exciting for Noah and his family to see the rainbow in the sky for the first time! It meant that the Flood was over and God would never send another!

Let's act!

Get a friend to help you with this one!

STEP 1

Pretend you are a news reporter reporting on the rainbow appearing for the first time. Choose one of you to play the reporter and one to play Noah's son or daughter-in-law.

STEP 2

Create a scene where you interview one of Noah's sons or daughters-in-law. You could ask questions such as:

» What was it like being stuck in a boat with your family for so long?

» Did you enjoy being on a boat with so many animals?

» When you saw the rainbow, how did you feel?

» Are you pleased about God's promise?

» Maybe you could think of more questions of your own too!

STEP 3

Rehearse your scene and perform it for an audience!

DROP BY DROP

It rained and it rained and it rained!
For 40 days and 40 nights it rained!
Yet God looked after Noah and his family.
God then promised that he would never send so much rain again, because he loves us and cares for us.

Let's get creative!

YOU WILL NEED:

white paper
different shades of blue paint
paintbrush
water
pencil

STEP 1 Create a raindrop picture by dripping a variety of shades of blue paint onto the page.

STEP 2 Draw large raindrop shapes around the drips.

STEP 3 Inside each large raindrop, write a word of a promise God gives us. You could use some of these words: peace, love, hope. Or choose words of your own.

love
peace
family
hope

KALEIDOSCOPIC HOPE

The rainbow that God sent was a sign of hope, a promise that he will never send a Flood like that again and that he will care for us and loves us.

A kaleidoscope is a toy that shows different patterns when you look through it. The patterns reflect the light, forming beautiful shapes that dance as the light hits them at different angles.

Let's get creative!

Why not create your own kaleidoscope light-catcher to remind you of the hope God gives us and his love for all his creation?

YOU WILL NEED:

a piece of see-through plastic
PVA glue
sticky tack
pieces of tissue paper

STEP 1 Cover your sheet of plastic in a thin layer of PVA glue.

STEP 2 Arrange your pieces of tissue paper in an irregular pattern. Be careful not to leave any gaps and to fill the sheet with your shapes. Leave to dry.

STEP 3 Once this is dry, paint another layer of PVA glue on top, this time a bit more thickly. Leave to dry! This stiffens the tissue paper and creates your kaleidoscope light catcher.

STEP 4 Once this is dry, peel off your paper design and stick onto a window using sticky tack.

STEP 5 Look at how the light shines through your paper and creates shapes on the walls and floor, reminding you of God's hope and love all around you.

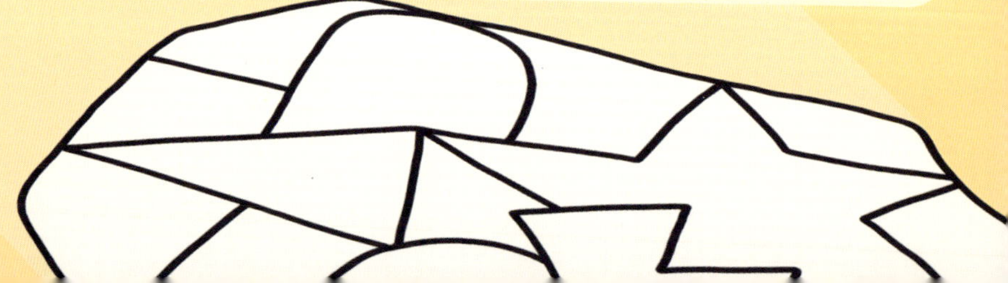

ON THE RIGHT TRACK

The world that God has created is made to fit together so well! The habitats (places) and how animals live alongside one another mean that the whole of creation works perfectly as a whole!

Let's get creative!

In the space below, draw as many different animal tracks as possible. You could draw insect trails, bear paw prints, or even the tracks that ducks leave behind. Get creative with seeing how many you can sketch.

Talk to an adult about what ecosystems (environments where animals and plants live and work together) you know about. What animals exist in them and how do they survive and thrive?

A Friend Near and Far!

God asks us to love everyone across the globe

MATTHEW 22:34–40

Jesus' friends asked him, "What's the most important rule?"
Jesus said, "Love your God with all your heart and soul!"
His friends nodded, listening to his every word:
Jesus said the wisest things that they had ever heard!
Although this was the greatest rule, Jesus said, "But wait! There's more!
Just as you love yourself, love your friend next door!"
So we need to love our God with all our soul and heart
And love other people as ourselves . . . but where do we start?!
Not just the person living on your street, but people far and near.
Family and friends, bus drivers, police officers, and even the shop cashier!
People listened carefully and remembered what Jesus had said.
They left their old ways of doing things and followed his instead . . .

Love others as yourself, and those in other countries,
not just your own.
And always love the Lord your God
who sits upon the throne!

Wow! That is an **awesome** rule for us to follow!

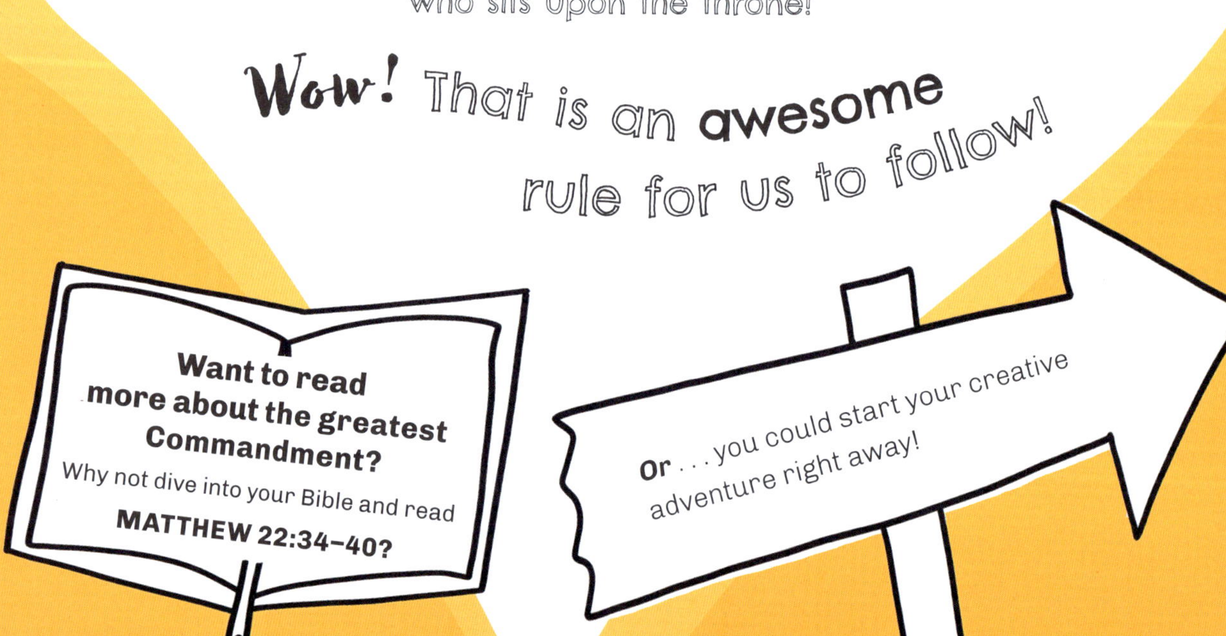

A.M. FOR ME IS P.M. FOR YOU

The different time zones in the world mean that, when it is the morning in the UK, it is the evening in Australia! That means that people across the globe are doing so many different things at the same point in the day!

DID YOU KNOW?

All over the world, the sun rises at different times because the earth is always in rotation.

This means that, at any one point in the day, there are 24 different time zones!

Let's get creative!

Make a "Prayer Time Wall" to prompt you to pray for people in different countries.

YOU WILL NEED:

two or more clocks or watches

STEP 1 On two clocks, set different times found in different time zones around the world.

STEP 2 Write the names of the countries in that time zone under the clock.

STEP 3 In the morning, pray for the people in those countries and what they may be doing at that time in the day, such as sleeping, working, or resting. Pray they will know that God is close to them.

STEP 4 In the evening, pray for them at that point in their day. Pray that God will bless their day ahead.

Wow! Time to pause ...

FOOD FOR THOUGHT

Where does the food that we get from the shops really come from? So much of the food is grown by farmers in different countries or produced in factories across the world! It is then flown or shipped to our country and delivered to the shops ready for us to buy!

Some food will have gone miles just to land in our basket, and so many people will have helped to grow and produce it for us!

Let's pause!

When you are in the supermarket, before you put food in your basket, have a look at where it was grown or packaged.

How far has it come?

Using an online map to help you, calculate the miles that your food has had to travel.

In the basket below, write down or draw all the people involved in helping you to get your food. For example, the farmer, the pilot, the packaging person.

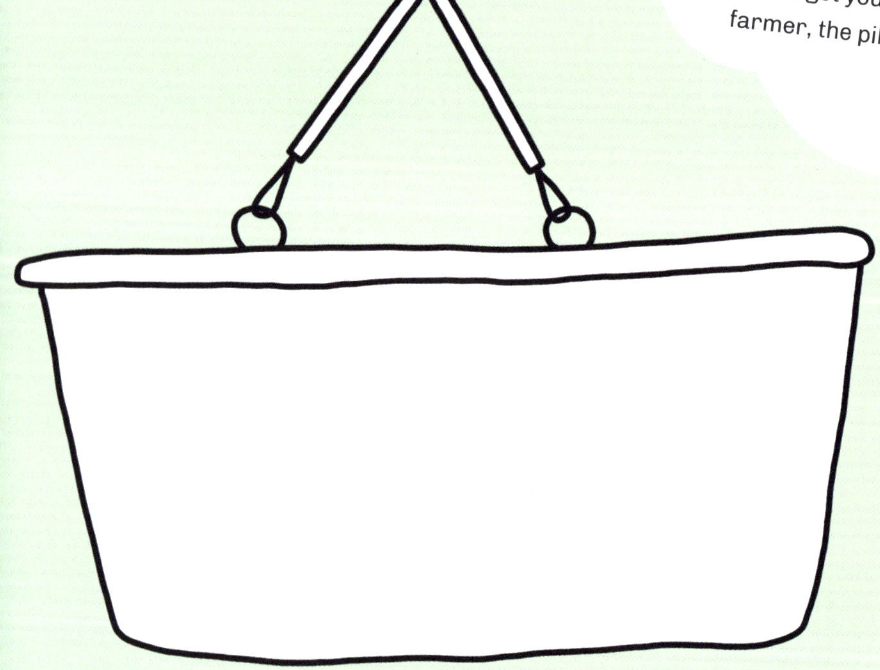

Thank God for their hard work and for the food he has given you.

WHERE TO NEXT?

There are SO many different cultures and communities across the globe! Many of them will have traditions, food, celebrations, and cities very different from our own!

Let's act!

Create an episode for a travel show pretending you're exploring a country. You will play the role of the travel-show presenter sharing the things you have discovered on your trip and telling the viewers about all the things they can see.

STEP 1

Research a country in the world that needs help. Find out about how people's lives have changed because of climate change. Gather as much information as possible.

STEP 2

Decide on a location for your show. It could be up a mountain, in the middle of a city, or inside a famous building.

STEP 3

Write down three facts you can share with the viewers on your TV show.

STEP 4

Rehearse your show, presenting the information about the country you have found out about. You could even pretend you are showing the views, landscape, or objects you're talking about.

STEP 5

Record your TV episode and show it back to an audience!

Wow! Let's create!

FLYING THE FLAG

There are hundreds of flags in the world, each one representing a country or nation and a whole group of people! That's a lot of different cultures and communities!

Sometimes we can forget this, and we don't realize the impact our actions can have on other countries. It could be that the plastic we throw away ends up in oceans close to another country in the world. Sometimes the fuels we use in our country are contributing to climate change, which is hugely damaging to living conditions on other continents in the world.

Let's get creative!

Make your own World Flag prayer bunting!

YOU WILL NEED:

paper
string
tape
pencil crayons
somewhere to be able to research the different flags of the world, such as a computer or library

STEP 1 Cut the paper into a number of large rectangular pieces.

STEP 2 Look up pictures of all the different flags of the world. Pick six flags of countries that have been impacted by flooding, drought, wildfires, or other effects of climate change.

STEP 3 Gather the pencils that you will need for each flag and draw each flag design to fill a whole sheet of rectangular paper.

STEP 4 Once you have completed your flag, use tape to stick the flags with the short side attached to the string.

STEP 5 Hang the flag bunting where you can see it. As you look at these flags, pray for each country to be protected and blessed by God. Ask God to help you to be wise in the decisions you make day to day and to consider how they may impact people across the world.

TOP TIP: **If you want to create more flags, you could ask friends to help you by designing different flags from yours and then join them together!**

YOU ARE AMAZING!

It's so wonderful that we have so many different cultures and people from different backgrounds in our country! Learning about what makes each of us different and unique and celebrating one another is one of the biggest joys in life.

Let's get creative!

Talk to a friend who comes from a different culture from you. Ask them questions about what the special things are in their community. Maybe you could ask them about their traditions, festivals, or even what their family is like?

Make a "You Are Amazing" card for them.

In the space, draw all the things that they told you about. Add in all the extra things that you think make them an awesome person.

Once you have created your design, copy it onto a separate piece of card and finish the design with stickers, pens, and paint.

Give them the "You Are Amazing" card to celebrate just how fantastic they are!

YOU ARE AMAZING!

FIRST-CLASS STAMP TO A FIRST-CLASS FRIEND

Having friends across the world is a really special thing! Although they may not be close by, they are still your friend and you can still love and care for them, just as God does.

Let's get creative!

Write a letter to a friend in another country. If you don't know anyone in a different country, you could see if a friend or adult does and you could write to their friend instead.

Talk to someone about what you could put in your letter, and note down some ideas in the shapes.

Seal the letter and put a stamp on it. As you post it, pray that God will give that person joy, that they will feel loved and blessed as they receive the letter.

TOP TIP: You could fill the letter with pictures of natural areas you like where you live! You could tell them about exciting things you do to look after God's creation or care for his animals. You could even let them know that you are praying for them and the environment they live in, too.

God's Epic Creation!

God created everything, so how do we care for his creation?

1 CHRONICLES 29:10–20

King David spoke out to the Lord in front of a huge crowd.
He wanted everyone to hear his prayer, so spoke out very loud.

"Praise to you, Oh my God! My father for evermore!
You are awesome, you're truly great, your power we can't ignore!
Everything in heaven and earth, it all belongs to you!
You rule over everything. This I know is true.
All the power on earth and all the wealth is yours.
You choose to give us our own strength, so struggles we can endure.
Now God, we give you all the thanks and all of our praise.
We will worship and choose to serve you for all of our days!"

If David said that everything was God's
and declared God's mighty power,
Does that change how we look after the world
and everything that's ours?
Shall we treat things with extra care
and pay attention to creation?
Yes, we will lift our praises loudly
in every country and each nation!

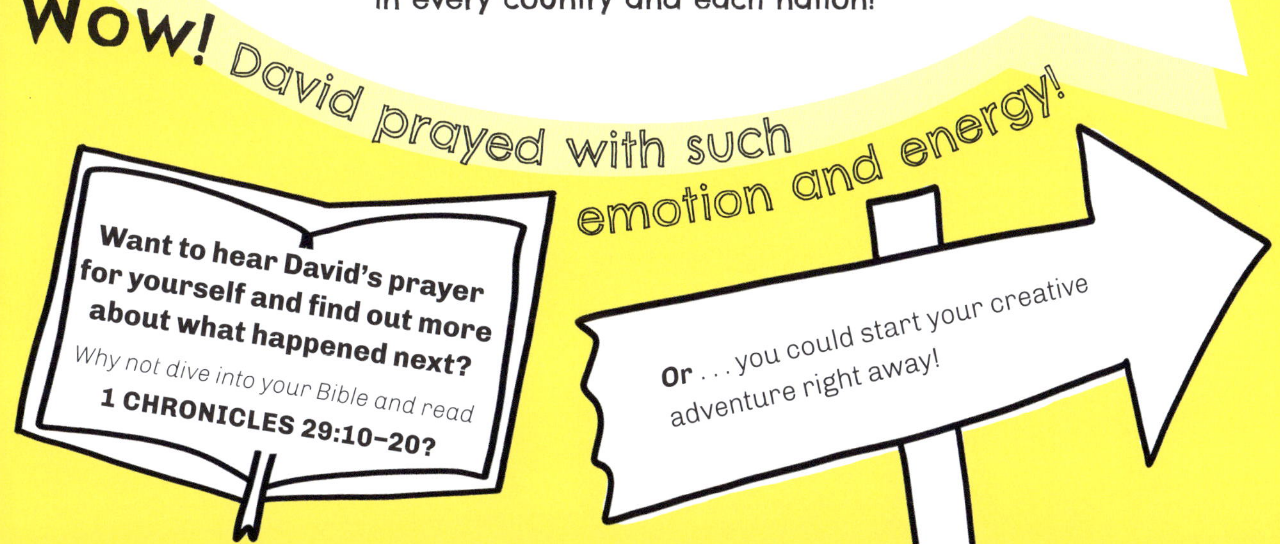

POSITIVE POST-IT PRAYERS

Do you think people spend more time complaining about what they *don't* like in their town, home, or school, or talking about what they *do* like? People are very quick to see the bad in things, but if everything is God's then surely it is good!

Let's get creative!

Why not make some "Positive Post-It Prayers", thanking God for all of the good things in your area. If someone spots one, it may help them to see the great things in your area too!

THANK YOU, GOD

PLEASE, GOD

YOU WILL NEED:

sticky notes or small pieces of bright paper
pens

STEP 1 Talk to someone about all the good things in your town, school, or community. Is it the parks, natural features, or even how friendly people are?

STEP 2 Draw or write each "good thing" on a sticky note. Fill the paper so it is bright and eye-catching!

STEP 3 Now talk about what things you would like to change or improve. Write or draw these "prayers of hope" on a sticky note too.

STEP 4 Stick the notes around your area in public places where people will see them. As you place the positive notes, say, "Thank You, God" for the good things he has given us. As you place the "prayers of hope", say, "Please, God", asking him to bless the area.

A GALAXY AND BEYOND

EVERYTHING belongs to God!

Everything on earth . . . the land, the sea, the animals, the people.

Everything in the sky . . . the clouds, the sun, the moon.

Even all the galaxies . . . the planets, the stars, and beyond!

Let's pause!

On a clear night, stand outside and look up at the stars.

As you stargaze, see how many different patterns of stars you can see. Can you spot any shooting stars?

How much smaller we seem when we see how much belongs to God. However, he still cares for us!

Draw in the spaces the patterns of stars you can see in the sky.

IT'S ALL YOURS!

The prayer of praise in Chronicles is by a king, called David, who loved God. He made it his mission to declare his prayer as loud as possible, so that everyone could hear what he was saying to God!

Can you imagine David standing in front of hundreds of people telling them just how amazing God is? He was probably very loud and expressive to show just how passionate he was about God!

Let's act!

STEP 1

Imagine you are David shouting your praise to God, proclaiming that everything is God's. Make your own prayer of praise by completing the gaps in the sentences.

STEP 2

When you have finished the script, stand tall, imagining you are David standing in front of a crowd wanting them to hear his prayer to God. Speak your script aloud with confidence in a loud voice, showing your passion to God.

STEP 3

Once you have rehearsed your prayer of praise, show it to someone. Don't forget to speak it loudly with passion!

God! I want to praise you forever!
Everything belongs to you!

My town

____

belongs to you.

My school

____

belongs to you.

In nature the

____

belong to you.

On earth the

____

belongs to you.

In space the

____

belong to you.

My friend

____

and I belong to you.

Everything belongs to you!
You are King over all!
I praise you because everything belongs to you!

UPCYCLE TO RECYCLE

If everything belongs to God, it is important that we don't waste or destroy things, but look after them as much as possible! This shows that we care about the things God has made and given us!

This includes keeping the possessions we've got and not just buying new things. We could upcycle and refresh the look of old things and find new uses for them.

DID YOU KNOW?

Nine hundred million items of clothing are sent to landfill in the UK each year!

Let's get creative!

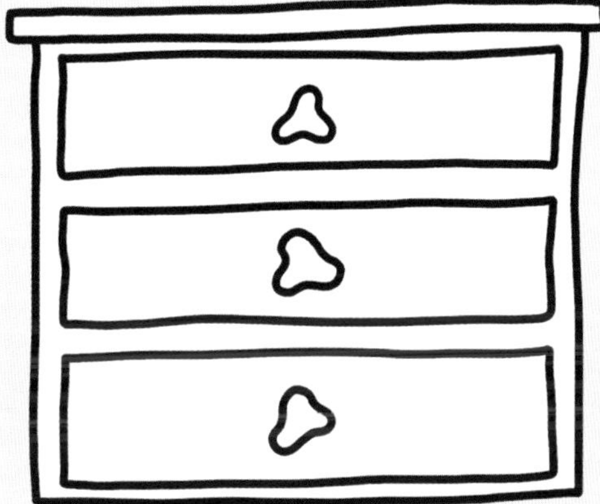

Find an item you may throw away. For example, a cushion, piece of clothing, broken or unused piece of furniture. How could you give it a new life by upcycling it?

Maybe you could sew a patch on a hole in your top or repaint where furniture is starting to look tatty?

Ask an adult to help you in your upcycling mission, and make sure you seek permission before upcycling anything!

LOVE LOCAL

In Chronicles, you can see that God gives David and the other workers the idea of building a temple and also gives them the talents and skills to do it!

This happens now too! God gives us talents and skills, and ideas of how to use them.

You can see people using their talents and skills everywhere in your local area!

The local bakery selling delicious bread handmade by the local baker!

A local gallery showing artwork handcrafted by a local artist.

Or even performances by musicians as you walk up your high street!

Let's get creative!

Create a "Love Local list" of ideas you could carry out to show God just how much you love and care for your local area, which is God's and which he loves too!

Love Local list!

» Support local businesses and people in your community by buying from local shops.

» Help others with jobs they may need doing.

» Pick up rubbish in your local park.

A BASKET **FULL**

It is amazing that we get the choice to support farmers and workers around the world, making sure they get fair treatment and fair pay for their work!

The best way we can do this is to remember that there are people who have grown and prepared the food for us before it landed in our basket, and to buy fair-trade food to make sure the farmers get fair pay.

Let's get creative!

Talk to someone about the food that you often buy from the shops.

Can you answer these questions?

» Who are the people who have grown the food?

» What country are they from?

» What makes the conditions in which they work fair?

It is their hard work that helps to sow, grow, and harvest the food! In the space below, decorate the picture of the farmer who has produced the fair-trade food. Finish the sentences in the spaces around the picture.

This smile is wide because . . .

. . . .

. . . .

These hands work hard by . . .

. . . .

. . . .

These feet tread ground that is . . .

. . . .

. . . .

Can you make some sentences of your own?

WOW!

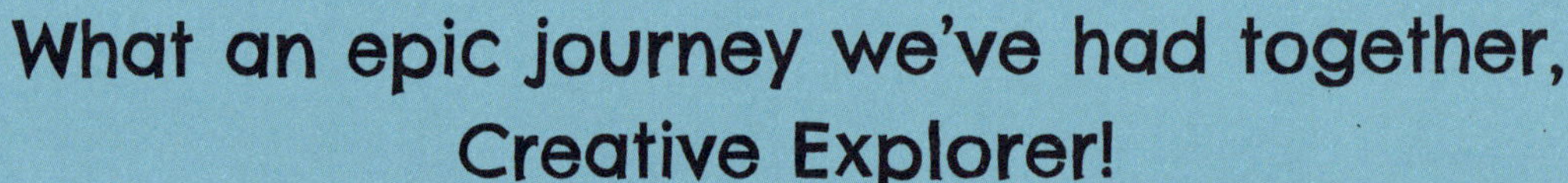

What an epic journey we've had together, Creative Explorer!

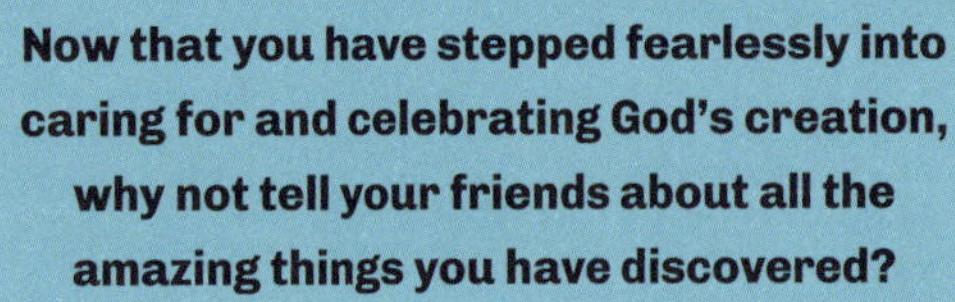

Now that you have stepped fearlessly into caring for and celebrating God's creation, why not tell your friends about all the amazing things you have discovered?

You could even show them some of the things you have created along the way!

The great thing is, you can use all these creative ideas again and again! They can be used on your own, in small groups, or in big groups!

The important thing is never to stop exploring, never to stop discovering new things, and of course never to stop having fun being creative!

Hope to see you again, Creative Explorer!

For more creative resources visit www.nimbuscollective.org
Also available:

WOW! JESUS
ISBN 978 1 78128 425 4

WOW! CHRISTMAS
ISBN 978 1 78128 424 7